This book is
your passport
into time.

Get ready to meet
Paul Revere.

Paul Revere and the Boston Tea Party

by Marc Kornblatt
illustrated by Ernie Colón

A Byron Preiss Book

A BANTAM SKYLARK BOOK®
TORONTO • NEW YORK • LONDON • SYDNEY • AUCKLAND

**To my parents,
Lloyd and Dolores,
who raised me
in this great country**

RL 3, 007-010

PAUL REVERE AND THE BOSTON TEA PARTY
A Bantam Skylark Book/September 1987

*Special thanks to Judy Gitenstein, Jim Walsh, Adrian Alperovich,
Carla Jablonski, Robin Stevenson, and Bruce Stevenson.*

*Book design by Alex Jay
Cover Painting by Ernie Colón
Cover design by Alex Jay
Mechanicals by Mary LeCleir
Typesetting by David E. Seham Associates, Inc.*

Editor: Ruth Ashby

*"Time Traveler" is a trademark of
Byron Preiss Visual Publications, Inc.*

*Skylark Books is a registered trademark of Bantam Books, Inc.
Registered in U.S. Patent and Trademark Office and elsewhere.*

ISBN 0-553-15529-6

Published simultaneously in the United States and Canada

PRINTED IN THE UNITED STATES OF AMERICA

0 9 8 7 6 5 4 3 2 1

Welcome, Time Traveler!

This book is your time machine. It is not like any book you've ever read. When you turn the page, you will travel back to one of the most exciting times in American history. You will meet Paul Revere, a leader in America's fight for freedom.

In every Time Traveler book you will be given a mission to complete while you are back in time. In this book you will be there at the Boston Tea Party.

Every few pages you will get to make a choice about what to do next. If you want help along the way, you can read the information about Revere in the next few pages.

 Now you're ready for your adventure. Turn the page and find out your mission!

Your Mission

Your mission is to meet the famous patriot Paul Revere and take part in America's fight for freedom. To fulfill your task, you must bring back one of the tomahawks used to crack open chests of tea during the Boston Tea Party.

Toward the end of the eighteenth century, America's thirteen colonies were eager to declare independence from Britain. A great turning point came on December 16, 1773, when a band of patriots disguised as Indians boarded three ships moored in Boston Harbor. Using tomahawks, they chopped apart 340 chests of British-taxed tea and threw them overboard.

Who actually took part in that event called the Boston Tea Party? Many feel that a secret club—the Sons of Liberty—organized the Tea Party. Legend has it that one of the group's leaders, Paul Revere, played an important role.

To complete your mission you will have to find Paul Revere, become a member of the Sons of Liberty, and be there at this historic event.

 To start the Time Machine, turn the page.

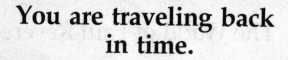

You are traveling back in time.

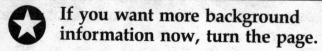

⭐ If you want more background information now, turn the page.

⭐ If you are ready to start your mission now, turn to page 1.

The World of Paul Revere

Before you start your mission, here is some information you'll need about Paul Revere and his time.

Most of us know about Paul Revere's midnight ride on April 18, 1775. Galloping through the sleepy villages of Massachusetts, he warned his countrymen of the advancing British Army. When the English redcoats arrived at the town of Lexington, the American minutemen were ready, and they met the British with loaded muskets. And so began the revolutionary war.

But Paul Revere contributed much more to his country than that famous ride in the night. A patriot and an artist, he was one of America's great citizens.

The son of a French silversmith, Paul Revere was born in Boston on January 1, 1735, and attended school through the sixth grade before becoming an apprentice in his father's shop.

Paul was nineteen and a skilled craftsman when his father died. As the oldest son, he became head of the family and supported his mother as well as his six brothers and sisters.

In spite of this large responsibility, the young man prospered. He married and became one of the finest silversmiths in America. He was also an important member of Boston's Sons of Liberty, a secret organization that helped to bring about the Revolution.

During Paul Revere's time, Boston was America's third largest city, with a busy seaport. Ships arriving there from the West Indies, Europe, and the Far East brought everything from molasses and oranges to glass and silk.

One of the most popular items was tea, which was imported to England from China. Though the Americans loved tea, many of them hated the idea of paying the British government any tax for the pleasure of drinking it. They believed their own government, rather than England's Parliament an ocean away, should have the power to collect taxes.

By Paul Revere's time, more and more people thought the thirteen British colonies had grown strong enough to form their own country totally separate from England.

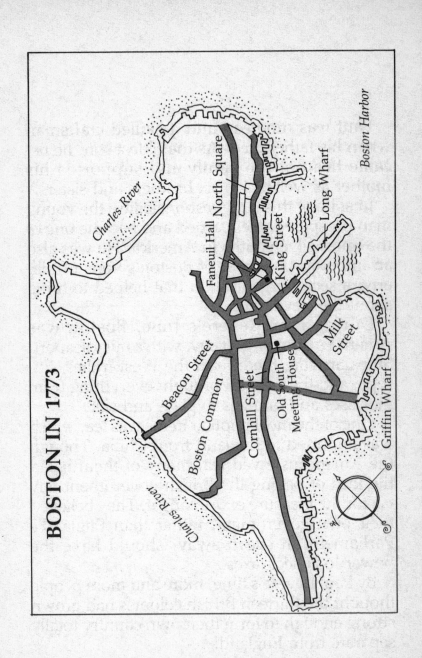

BOSTON IN 1773

Charles River

Boston Harbor

Long Wharf

Faneuil Hall

North Square

King Street

Milk Street

Beacon Street

Cornhill Street

Boston Common

Old South Meeting House

Charles River

Griffin Wharf

These independent-minded citizens called themselves Whigs. Their opponents, who remained loyal to traditional British rule, were known as Tories.

When three ships carrying British-taxed tea arrived in Boston during the autumn of 1773, a number of Whigs, such as Paul Revere and his fellow Sons of Liberty, decided it was time for a showdown.

 Now you are ready to begin your adventure. Turn the page.

It's November 28, 1773, just before noon. You're standing in the middle of the pier of Boston's Long Wharf. Large sailing ships are moored on one side, and shops and warehouses line the other side. Men wearing white wigs and three-cornered hats jostle you as they pass.

"Fine oysters!" shouts a fisherman in front of his boat. "Fresh haddock!" yells another.

As you head down the noisy pier, the smells of limes, tar, and fish fill your nostrils.

Suddenly, a gray cat comes running toward you. It is being chased by a snapping bull terrier. A merchant shouts angrily as the animals knock over his basket of raisins. "Stop that hound!" cries a young man scrambling after them.

Acting quickly, you lunge for the dog as it passes. The muscular terrier is very strong, but you manage to hold onto it. The cat flees into a cobbler's shop.

"Thank you," says the dog's owner, walking

up to you. He takes the struggling terrier from your arms. "Settle down now, Solly." He pats its big, bony muzzle.

The man offers you his hand. "I'm George Robert Twelves Hewes." Dressed in tight yellow breeches and a black coat with shiny buttons, he resembles a circus ringmaster. You tell him your name.

"You realize you've just saved Solomon the Wise, the smartest dog in America, don't you?" the man says grandly.

Hewes turns to find the angry raisin seller standing before him. Smiling broadly, he reaches into his pocket and pulls out a coin. "Forgive us. Cats are Solly's only folly," he says, handing the money to the merchant. "But allow me to treat you both to a demonstration."

You're eager to find Paul Revere. But before you can move, spectators crowd around from every side.

Solly is very well trained. Upon command he plays dead, rolls over, and stands on his hind legs. "Not bad. But can he fight?" asks a tall sailor.

"My good man," replies Hewes, "Solly here is not a brawler. He's a talker."

"That's blarney!" another man scoffs.

"No, it's fact! And for a small fee I'd be happy

to prove it," says Hewes, passing around his hat. Some men toss in coins.

Pocketing the money, Hewes picks up his terrier. "Now, Solly, tell me." The dog stares its master in the eye. "What is the opposite of smooth?" Solly cocks his head. "Ruff!" he barks.

"Precisely! The opposite of smooth is rough!" The spectators laugh. "Now," Hewes continues, "what's on top of a house?" Solly again cocks his head as if thinking. "Ruff!"

"Correct! A roof!" Solly jumps to the ground and dances around on his hind legs like a proud schoolboy.

Everyone cheers, including you. Any dog can make noises that sound like *rough* or *roof*. But Solly does it so intelligently it's fun to watch.

As Hewes and Solly bow before their appreciative audience, a blond-haired boy appears, carrying a stack of handbills.

"Friends! Countrymen!" he yells. "The taxed tea from England has arrived!"

The cheering stops, and the boy's papers are snatched up and read at once.

"I may like my tea, but I won't pay an unfair tax for the right to drink it!" shouts one man.

"We should be able to vote on our own taxes in Parliament, like any other Englishmen," adds another.

You manage to catch a glimpse of one of the handbills. "Meet at Faneuil Hall, at nine o'clock tonight," it says.

Surely, Paul Revere and the other Sons of Liberty will be at that meeting.

 Jump ahead ten hours to Faneuil Hall. Turn to page 11.

You approach the man on the horse. "Excuse me, are you Mr. Revere?"

"I am." He has a friendly smile. "I'd be happy to talk with you, but right now I'm in a hurry. I'm sorry, but please stand back."

With that, Revere spurs his horse and canters away.

You've met Paul Revere, but you need to find him when he's not on the move. You approach the man who was talking with the silversmith. "Do you know where Mr. Revere is going?"

He shakes his head. "Can't say. Bold Paul's always dashing somewhere."

"Well, where does he live?" you ask.

"North Square," the man says. "Go straight down Ann Street until it turns into Fish, and you'll run right into it."

"Where's Ann Street?"

"You're standing on it." He smiles. "Just visiting, are you?"

"Uh, yes." You thank the man and hurry on.

 Turn to page 19.

You find yourself in a dense forest. The air smells sweet, and the only sound you hear is that of the breeze as it sways the branches of the surrounding fir trees.

Seeing a brook up ahead, you walk to it and kneel down for a drink. You didn't realize how thirsty you were. The water tastes great.

Plunk! Something splashes in front of you. Maybe it's a fish or a frog. You look into the rippling water to find out.

A strange young face stares back at you! "Hello," it says. You gasp in surprise. Then you realize the face is a reflection. It belongs to a young girl with long black hair. "Forgive me if I startled you," she adds with a smile.

You straighten up to face her. "I thought I was alone," you say. The girl wears animal skins and moccasins. She looks like an Indian princess. "Have you lost your way to the settlement at Plymouth?" she asks.

Plymouth? She must think you're a Pilgrim. You've jumped back 150 years into the past.

"I only stopped for a drink and a short rest," you reply.

"My name is Golden Sunset," she says. "I've been fishing with my brother and father downstream. Would you like to join us?"

Fishing with this friendly Indian girl and her family would be fun. But you still must join a group of *make-believe* Indians—at the Boston Tea Party.

"I wish I could, but I must return to where I came from," you tell the girl. "Good-bye."

You leave her by the brook and jump ahead to finish the job you started for the printers Edes and Gill.

 Turn to page 38.

It's nine o'clock in the evening, and the sound of church bells is heard through the air. Thousands of excited people fill the narrow streets of Boston.

You join the mob, which is flowing like a giant wave toward Faneuil Hall. Everybody is talking about the three ships from England.

"The *Dartmouth*'s already docked at Griffin Wharf. The *Beaver* and the *Eleanor* are due any day now," a man tells a woman walking beside him.

"Together they're carrying ninety thousand pounds of tea," he adds. "And the king says we must pay tax on every ounce!"

"It's not enough that I let three of his soldiers sleep in my house at no charge to save the king money," says the woman. "Now I have to pay extra to drink Britain's tea."

"We won't buy a cup's worth," the old man vows.

In the heart of the city you find Faneuil Hall. It is filled to capacity. Inside, the meeting is already going on.

"Tyranny is staring us all in the face!" you hear a man with a high voice exclaim. "We must fight it!"

"Who's that speaking?" you ask a young woman next to you.

"It's Sam Adams, one of the Whig leaders," she replies.

Good. He must be connected to the Sons of Liberty. You're in the right place. You hear Adams call for a vote. "All those in favor of sending that cursed tea back to England."

"Aye!" everyone shouts in unison.

"It's settled. Meeting adjourned," Adams announces. People stream out of Faneuil Hall. You catch sight of the boy who was passing out handbills on Long Wharf. He seems to know his way around. Maybe he can point out Paul Revere. You start toward him to ask for advice when you hear a voice behind you.

"What happens next, Paul?" the voice says. You turn to see two men standing beside a brown horse.

"We wait. England may reconsider," one of them says. He's stocky, rosy-cheeked, and he wears no wig. Could this man actually be Paul Revere?

The stocky man mounts the horse. Should you run to ask him his name, or go talk to the boy? Decide quickly, or soon they'll both be gone.

 Do you want to run after the man? Turn to page 7.

 Do you want to speak to the boy? Turn to page 26.

The still night air makes you drowsy, and you fight to stay awake as you wait for Paul Revere's daughter. "Eleven o'clock and all's well," announces a town crier carrying a lantern as he walks across North Square.

Someone touches you on the shoulder. It's the girl. "Hello. I'm Sara," she tells you with a smile. "Are you a friend of the Sons of Liberty?"

"Yes," you answer.

"My stepmother probably thought you were too young, but I don't."

"What happens if your stepmother catches you out of the house?" you ask.

"Don't worry. She sleeps like a log."

You run with Sara back to the center of town. Faneuil Hall and Long Wharf are both closed up for the night. The streets are empty.

The two of you stop to catch your breath on King Street. A few doors down, a coffeehouse is still open. A fierce-looking British soldier steps into the doorway and spots you.

"What do you want?" he asks with a sneer.

"Nothing, thank you," replies Sara.

"Then off with you!"

Sara ignores him and continues on with you by her side. "That bully!" she says. "The redcoats were sent here to help keep the peace. But they pick fights instead."

Arriving at Griffin Wharf, you see a tall-masted ship moored at the end of the pier.

"That's the *Dartmouth*," she explains. Looking down the wharf, you see a group of men standing by the boat. They're carrying lanterns and cradling muskets in their arms as they pace slowly back and forth. "The Sons of Liberty are preventing the British tea from being unloaded," says Sara.

"I'd better go now. If my father catches me, I'll be in trouble. He's even stricter than Rachel." Sara wishes you luck and hurries off.

You head down Griffin Wharf toward the *Dartmouth*. Two men immediately bar your way. "Halt! Who goes there?" one shouts. You recognize him in the dim light coming from his companion's lantern. It's Paul Revere—and he's aiming his musket at your chest!

"I've come to help the Sons of Liberty," you blurt out.

Seeing your face, Revere lowers his gun. "This is adults' work," he says. "Don't you realize it's dangerous around here?"

"Yes, but—"

"You'd better go home before you get hurt," he orders.

You hesitate, but you realize Paul Revere is the last person you want to have as an enemy.

You decide to jump back three hours to Faneuil Hall and find the boy who had the handbills. Maybe you can work your way into the Sons of Liberty through him.

 Turn to page 26.

You reach North Square and discover that it's not a square at all. It's a long, narrow, cobblestone triangle rimmed by small houses. The street is quiet; most of the homes are dark.

You see a friendly-looking two-story house with a candle burning in one of its downstairs windows and decide to ask about Paul Revere there. A handsome woman answers your knock.

"Sorry to bother you, ma'am," you say politely. "But could you please tell me where I might find the home of Paul Revere?"

"This is it. I'm Rachel Revere. But what do you want here at this time of night?"

"I'd like to speak with your husband."

She shakes her head. "He's not home, but you should be. Don't you know it's past ten?"

"Yes, but it's important," you insist.

"Come back tomorrow," she says. "All six children in this house are sound asleep. That's what you should be, too."

Mrs. Revere shuts the door, leaving you outside. Now what?

"Pssst!" You hear a sound from above. Looking up, you see a dark-haired girl about your age wave from a second-story window of the Revere house. "I know where my father is," she whispers. "Wait by the water pump in the middle of the square. After my mother goes to sleep I'll take you to him."

Mrs. Revere may not go to bed for a while. Should you wait for her daughter to sneak out of the house, or should you return to Faneuil Hall and find the boy you first saw at Long Wharf?

 Do you want to wait for Paul Revere's daughter? Turn to page 15.

 Do you want to go back and find the boy? Turn to page 26.

It's March 26, 1770, three years before the Boston Tea Party. You're standing in the middle of Dassett Alley. Somewhere along this narrow, dirty street is the shop of Edes and Gill.

"Look out!" A man on a horse is coming straight at you! There's no sidewalk to hop onto for safety, so you flatten yourself against the front of a building as the animal and rider brush by.

The rider looked familiar, but you're not sure who it was. He passed too quickly. You continue down the street until you find a sign: *Edes and Gill, Printers of the* **Boston Gazette.**

You enter the shop to find a tall, strong man working at a large, wooden-framed machine.

"*Umph!*" Using two hands, he cranks a handle to turn a thick screw attached to an iron plate. "*Umph!*" The heavy plate bears down upon a metal frame mounted on a table, and the man lets it rest there for a moment.

Soon he notices you. "Don't just stand there. You look as if you've never seen a hand press

before," the man says, wiping his brow. His voice is deep but gentle.

"I haven't," you reply.

"Well, come closer then." The man cranks the handle in the opposite direction and raises the iron plate. Then he removes a sheet of paper from the frame beneath it. On the paper is a picture of British soldiers shooting at a peaceful crowd. Five people lie dead on the ground. Above them are written the words: *The Bloody Massacre, March 5, 1770.*

"John Gill!" calls the man. "Come see the engraving that Paul Revere just delivered. I've inked it up and pressed it." Paul Revere? He must have been the rider who almost ran you down before on the street.

A thin man wearing glasses enters the workshop from a side room. He squints to study the tiny print. "Paul's a better silversmith than engraver, but this will help show the people what evil Britain can do," John Gill says. "Let's sell copies of it."

Benjamin Edes nods and looks at you. "Do you want to help?"

"Yes," you reply eagerly.

"Good!" He slaps you on the shoulder. His powerful hand smells of ink.

Edes presses ten more prints of Paul Revere's

engraving. "Ask for eight pence each. If some- one doesn't have the whole amount, take what you can get," he instructs you. "Come back for more as soon as you sell out."

As soon as the ink is dry, you tuck the prints under your arm and leave the shop.

Selling prints for Edes and Gill may be a good way to gain their confidence, but it may also be a waste of time. Maybe you should go to the site of the Boston Massacre. If Paul Revere made an engraving of the scene, you may learn something important there.

 Do you want to sell Edes and Gill's prints? Turn to page 38.

 Do you want to go to the Boston Massacre? Turn to page 28.

You push your way through the crowd at Faneuil Hall to reach the blond-haired boy you saw passing out the handbills.

"Hello," you say. "Can we talk for a moment?"

The boy looks you up and down. "Come on," he replies. You follow him to a quieter spot, where you introduce yourself.

"I'm Joshua Wyeth," the boy says. "You look familiar. Were you in the Common last winter when we met the redcoats?"

You hesitate, unsure of what to answer.

"The day of the big fight," he adds.

Big fight? That sounds important. "A lot has happened since then," you reply.

"Truly," he agrees, "but I'll never forget that day. We have to teach those British a lesson."

You make a note to yourself to find out about the fight in the Common. Then, switching subjects, you say, "I was on Long Wharf today when you dropped off your handbills, and I was wondering who gave them to you."

"Why?" he asks suspiciously. "You aren't a Tory working for the redcoats, are you?"

"No. I support the Sons of Liberty."

"Well, that's a different story," he says. "My

masters, Benjamin Edes and John Gill, printed the handbills. Their shop's in Dassett Alley behind the State House. They publish the *Boston Gazette*, the Whig newspaper."

If Edes and Gill are connected with the Whigs, they may also be members of the Sons of Liberty. Working for them could prove useful. "Do your masters need any extra help?" you ask.

"No. I've been with them for two years, and I have another five before I finish my apprenticeship," Joshua replies. "Now I'd better get back before I'm locked out for the night." He tips his cap to you and hurries on.

Edes and Gill may be good contacts. Perhaps you can jump back before Joshua's apprenticeship began and offer your services to them. That way you won't interfere with Joshua's apprenticeship later on.

Or maybe you should find out what happened at the Common last winter. It may have been an important event.

 Do you want to jump back in time to the Common? Turn to page 35.

 Do you want to jump back in time and meet Edes and Gill? Turn to page 22.

You find yourself on a gloomy side street in early evening, March 5, 1770. Slush and ice cover the ground. You feel chilled.

Out of the dark, a group of men and boys dash down the street toward you. "Drive out the redcoats!" someone cries. One of the boys tugs your sleeve as he passes. "To the King Street Customs House." You run with him.

On King Street you join a small crowd gathered in front of the Customs House. A lone British sentry stands guard on the steps in front of the building.

The boy who pulled you along walks up to him. "Why haven't you paid my father for the boots he made you?" he asks accusingly. "Don't the British pay their debts?"

"Shut up!" the soldier yells, striking him with his musket butt. Holding his head, the boy shrieks in pain and hurries away.

The crowd surges in upon the sentry. "Bloody-back!" men shout, pointing at his blood-red coat.

Aiming his musket at them, the soldier warns, "Come near me and I'll blow you to smithereens."

Church bells ring loudly as more townspeople appear, swelling the crowd in front of the Customs House to the size of an angry mob.

You struggle to find a safer spot off to one side. In the bright moonlight you see that many of the townspeople are armed with pitchforks and swords.

"Hang the redcoats! Drive them out!" voices chant.

The surly sentry looks like a trapped animal.

"Make way!" Eight British soldiers push through to their comrade. Forming a semicircle, they level their muskets at the shouting people.

"Disperse!" orders the captain of the guard.

The people answer him with curses and snowballs.

"Come on, lobsters," calls out a young man, making fun of the soldiers' uniforms. "I dare you to shoot!"

"Disperse!" the captain demands again.

A tall black man shakes a thick club. "We're not afraid of you."

More snowballs and stones rain down upon the redcoats.

Someone hurls a club. It grazes the captain's

shoulder, then hits one of his men and knocks him to the ground.

Frantically, the fallen soldier rises and fires, hitting the black man. *"Ugh!"* The wounded man drops in a pool of blood.

The other soldiers fire. *Crack! Crack!* More people in the crowd fall.

Crack! The man beside you topples over. You've seen enough. Jump for your life!

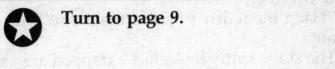

Turn to page 9.

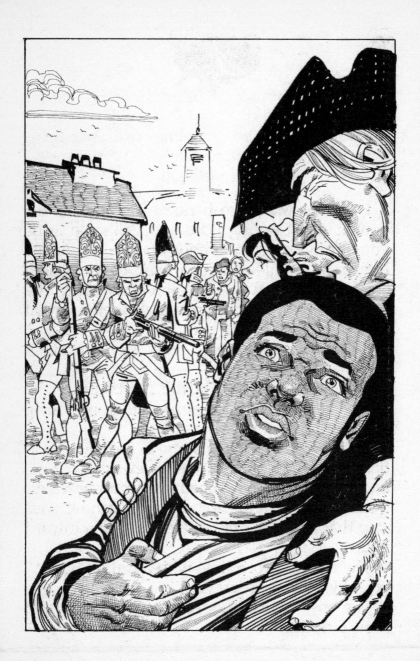

Ebenezer Mackintosh doesn't bother to ask your name. Leaving Edes and Gill's, he leads you through a neighborhood of neat, handsome homes to a foul-smelling section of town with crooked streets and run-down tenements. The people here seem poor; some of them stare at you with mean, hard eyes.

"Where are we going?" you ask Mackintosh nervously.

"To my shoe shop in the North End," he says. His abrupt tone keeps you from asking any more questions.

The North End streets are in terrible condition. There are huge potholes every few feet, and most of them are filled with muddy water. You're concentrating so hard on watching your step that you don't notice a boy coming toward you.

The two of you collide with a thud. "Sorry," you say. "I didn't see you."

The boy scowls. "Looked to me as if you did it on purpose."

"No, it was an accident," you assure him.

"Well, I don't believe you," he replies, folding his arms across his chest and barring your path.

"But it's true," you insist.

The boy shoves you by the shoulder. "And I said I don't believe you." It seems he's challenging you to a fight.

You look at Mackintosh, who's standing a short way up the street. He is smiling and watching you closely, while waiting to see what you'll do.

This bully is only an inch or two taller than you, but he's a great deal wider. And he looks strong.

The boy is preparing to shove you again. Should you stand up to him, or retreat?

 Do you want to stand up to the boy? Turn to page 44.

 Perhaps you should *not* fight. Turn to page 43.

It's a cold February day on the Boston Common. It's 1773.

You're standing at the bottom of a snow-covered hill that looks out over a large field. The frosty air makes you shiver. Dusk is approaching.

You hear loud voices coming from the other side of the hill. You decide to investigate. "Go, Thomas!" you hear someone yell. "Beat him, Josh!" shouts another voice.

A group of youngsters watches as two boys sled down the hill. All of a sudden one of the racers hits a bump and goes flying. *"Ooooff!"* He lands in the snow with a thud as his runaway sled slides to a stop at your feet.

You bring the sled back to him. The boy is Joshua Wyeth, looking about a year younger than when you last saw him. "Thanks," he says. "You can have a ride if you like." This is really your first meeting, so he doesn't recognize you.

You accept his offer just as a band of well-armed British troops appears and marches across the boys' sledding path.

"Say! You're ruining our trail!" the boys cry. Ignoring them, the soldiers tread on.

"What's wrong with those redcoats?" shouts the biggest boy of the group. "Is the Common so small that they have to trample our spot?" He makes a snowball. "Come on!" The boys charge after the soldiers. You follow.

You run fast, catching up to the soldiers at the edge of the Common. "Take that!" the boys yell, pelting the men with snowballs.

"You'll get yours, rascals!" bellows one of the men. He and another soldier stop and grab thick icicles hanging from a tree. Hurling them the men hit a small boy in the head.

The boy's face turns nearly as red as the men's coats as he struggles to keep from crying.

The two soldiers laugh and unsheath their swords. Shaking them threateningly, they shout, "Be gone!"

All of the boys scatter. You run behind some fir trees.

Britain's unfair taxation is not the only thing that upsets America's colonists. Its soldiers cause trouble here as well.

You decide to go to the printing shop of Edes and Gill, where you might be able to track down the Sons of Liberty.

 Turn to page 22.

Carrying the prints Paul Revere made of the Boston Massacre, you hurry to the center of town. "A *Boston Gazette* special!" you call out. "Eight pence apiece!"

People rush to buy Paul Revere's engraving, and his picture of British troops shooting peaceful citizens enrages them. "Villains!" hisses one man. "We'll show those redcoats," another promises.

"Hello, friend," says a man with a familiar smile. "My funds are low. Would you accept sixpence?" He doesn't know you yet, because the last time you met was in 1773, three years in the future. But you recognize George Robert Twelves Hewes by his grand manner.

"Happy to oblige," you reply.

The discounted print you give George Hewes is your last one. Revere's prints have sold like hotcakes! With the money you've collected jingling in your pocket, you return to Edes and Gill's. There you find Benjamin Edes talking to a husky stranger.

"Here's eighty-six pence for the eleven prints you gave me." You hand Edes the change. "I sold one copy for sixpence."

"Well done," the printer says, clapping you on the back. He offers you a few of the coins. "Come back later and we may have more work for you."

"You don't have to pay me," you say boldly. "I did it to help the Sons of Liberty."

Benjamin laughs heartily. "You hear that, Ebenezer?" he says to the stranger. "We have a young patriot before us."

Ebenezer says nothing. Instead, he stares at you long and hard. "Maybe we can use someone like you," he remarks at last. "Then again, you may be too young."

Even though he makes you feel uneasy, this tough-looking man could be important. "Give me a chance," you tell him. "I'll do my best."

Ebenezer glances toward Benjamin Edes, who says, "My dear Mackintosh, what more can you ask?"

Ebenezer Mackintosh shrugs and moves toward the door. "Come on, imp," he says, beckoning.

You go with him.

 Turn to page 32.

You're alone on a beach beside an emerald sea. The memory of falling into the Boston pothole makes you wince in shame.

To dry your clothes, you lie down on a white stretch of sand. Mmmm, the sun feels good. You let yourself drop into a soothing sleep and dream about winning a fight with the boy from the North End.

"Ahoy there!" a distant voice calls. Is it real or a dream? You open your eyes. "Ahoy!" The voice sounds louder; it must be real.

You rub your eyes and stretch. Looking out, you see three tall ships anchored in the water. Men in a rowboat are pulling toward shore.

They could be pirates! You hide in the shadows of a palm tree grove and watch as they land and step proudly onto the beach.

"I name this island San Salvador on behalf of King Ferdinand and Queen Isabella of Spain," says one of the men. He plants a red and white flag in the sand, while the others cheer.

Several red-skinned men dressed in loincloths

walk past your hiding place toward the new arrivals. The man with the flag bows to them. "I am Christopher Columbus, commander of this expedition," he says.

You feel as if you're still dreaming. You are witnessing Christopher Columbus's discovery of America.

"I have come to the East Indies to trade for gold and spices," he tells the island people.

The men in loincloths look puzzled. They don't seem to understand what Columbus is talking about.

Columbus believes he has landed in the East Indies, but you know he's in the Bahamas. Unfortunately, you can't explain that to him. This may be a great moment in history, but you have to complete your mission.

To do that, you'll have to win Ebenezer Mackintosh's respect. Jump back to Boston's North End and stand up to the boy who challenged you to a fight.

 Turn to page 44.

Studying the boy, you see that he looks like an experienced street brawler. He has a purple welt under his right eye and scabby knuckles.

It isn't worth fighting him in order to prove yourself to Ebenezer Mackintosh. You'd rather find another way into the ranks of the Sons of Liberty.

"I'm very sorry, but I must be going," you tell the boy. You turn and run.

Splash! You forgot about the potholes, and you've fallen right into one filled with dirty water! You're soaked and filthy.

"Hah, hah, hah!" Mackintosh and the boy both laugh as you pick yourself up.

Feeling ridiculous, you scurry into a darkened alley and jump.

 Turn to page 40.

"Stop pushing me," you tell the boy. "I've apologized for bumping into you. What else am I to do?"

The boy grins nastily. "I'll show you." Clenching his fists, he lunges at you. But, although the boy may be stronger, you're quicker. You dodge out of his way and trip him as he lumbers by.

Splash! Your attacker stumbles into a pothole full of dark brown water. "Hah, hah, hah," says Ebenezer Mackintosh, laughing. You smile too; the boy is a muddy mess.

He jumps out of the pothole. "I'll teach you!" The boy attempts to charge again, but Ebenezer steps between the two of you. "Go home and dry off, Eli," he orders. After giving you an evil look, Eli stalks off, his boots dripping dirty water.

"Not bad," says Ebenezer, nodding. "Come on."

Mackintosh leads you down a side street to his cobbler's shop, which is filled with shoes.

You watch him nail new heels to a pair of brocade slippers and fix a spur on a riding boot. "Time to make the rounds," the shoemaker says as soon as his work is done.

You go with Ebenezer to return the finished shoes. Along the way he sends you into certain shops to deliver a secret message: "The Green Dragon. Tonight at eight."

You wonder what the message means, but having already learned that Mackintosh doesn't like questions, you keep quiet.

It's dark by the time the two of you stop outside a brick tavern. On the front of the building hangs a large copper lizard discolored by rust— a green dragon!

The tavern air smells of tobacco. Mackintosh orders a flagon of beer and roast veal for himself. He buys you a meat pie and a mug of cider. "Stay near," he orders. "I might need you to run an errand."

Eating your dinner at the bar, you watch the shoemaker greet several of the people to whom you delivered his message earlier. A sloppy, gray-haired man enters the Green Dragon, and people hurry up to shake his hand. He seems to know everyone, including Mackintosh.

"Gentlemen, let's move to the back for our meeting," he says in a high-pitched voice.

You know that voice. You heard it on the day the British-taxed tea arrived in Boston. The man is Sam Adams, the Whig leader who proposed sending the tea back to England.

The Boston Tea Party may be three years away, but staying in 1770 has paid off. You've apparently found a Sons of Liberty gathering place.

You're about to follow Sam Adams into a back room when a man bursts into the tavern. It's Paul Revere! "There's a fire on Cornhill Street!" he cries. He runs out, and immediately everyone rushes after him.

You've finally found Paul Revere and the Sons of Liberty together, but it's at a moment of great confusion. Should you help them fight the fire or jump ahead to a less dangerous time?

 Do you want to jump ahead?
Turn to page 52.

 Should you help fight the fire?
Turn to page 48.

In an emergency, an extra pair of hands can make the difference between life and death!

You run with the people who are rushing out of the Green Dragon tavern and race with them past Faneuil Hall to Cornhill Street.

There, a wooden house is burning out of control. The heat coming from it makes the air feel like an oven.

"Keep it steady!" shouts Paul Revere, his white shirt soaked in sweat. He fills leather buckets with water from a hand pump and passes them down a long line of men and women. Four people at the end of the line take turns pouring water on the flames.

To your astonishment, a band of British soldiers drives up on a wagon carrying a huge barrel filled with water.

"Let's make a second line!" one of the soldiers shouts. It seems the redcoats weren't always unfriendly.

You join the new line. But neither your help nor the soldiers' is enough to conquer the raging

fire. The flames spread to the neighboring wooden homes.

A woman carrying a child runs from one of the burning houses. Her anguished scream pierces the air. "My baby!"

People run to her aid. "My other daughter is upstairs," she says, sobbing. "The steps inside caught fire before I could reach her!"

Men try to enter the woman's house, but roaring flames in the doorway drive them back.

"She's in there," cries the woman, pointing to a small second-story window.

Paul Revere climbs on top of a tall soldier's shoulders and pushes open the window. But he's too big to fit through its narrow frame.

An idea hits you, and you hurry to him. "Maybe I can squeeze inside," you say.

Paul Revere's eyes flash with hope. "It's worth a try."

He lifts you onto the tall soldier's back, and you manage to just grab hold of the windowsill. "Careful, now," warns Paul. "We don't want to lose you, either."

As you pull yourself inside, the heat and smoke in the room almost stop you. You hold your sleeve across your mouth to keep from choking.

In the middle of the floor lies a little girl, unconscious. Fighting through the thick smoke, you pick her up and carry her to the open window. She's as limp as a rag doll.

"Bless you," says Paul Revere as you gently drop the girl into his waiting arms below. He smiles in admiration; people on the street cheer.

You're about to climb out the window when a ceiling beam crashes down and knocks you to the floor. *Whomp!* It missed crushing you by inches!

Your escape is cut off, and the heat is unbearable! Jump before you pass out!

 Jump ahead ten hours. Turn to page 59.

You're standing on the edge of a thick green lawn as a light rain falls. It's cold and gloomy out, making it difficult to see very far in front of you.

Suddenly, a man carrying a musket steps out from behind a nearby bush. Seeing you, he nods and goes to join a group of other armed men gathering quietly on the lawn.

In the distance you hear a faint slapping noise. It sounds like people marching.

You watch as the men on the lawn form a scraggly line. "Hold firm, brothers," someone in the group says as the marching sound grows louder. "Now is the time to show the British that we are free men."

An early dawn light breaks through the fog. Now you can make out a low wall around the lawn and the outline of a surrounding town. Beyond the lawn is a road. The slapping sound is a column of British redcoats marching toward you!

The English soldiers halt. There is a moment of eerie silence.

"Throw down your weapons and no harm will come to you," a British voice calls out to the men lined up on the lawn.

"Never!" shout the men, raising their muskets.

Crack! A gun goes off, and one of the men on the lawn falls. More shots ring out. *"Ahhh!"* someone screams, as you dive for cover behind the stone wall.

Crack! Crack! You meant to jump to a safe moment in history. Instead, you find yourself in the middle of a battle. You'd better jump away, or your mission may end here!

But wait! The shooting has stopped. You peek from behind your hiding place and see the British soldiers marching off.

Springing over the wall, you race toward the nearest fallen man. "Sir, are you hurt badly?"

He smiles at you, stands, and brushes himself off. "Looked like the real thing, didn't it?" he says.

Two of the other fallen men rise and dust themselves off. You're surprised to see that no one is stained with blood.

"What's going on?" you ask the first man.

"The fight here on Lexington Green is over," he explains. "If you hurry, you can see the second mock battle at Concord."

Mock battle? You still don't understand. "Do you mean you were only pretending?"

Some of the soldiers laugh.

"Don't make fun. It happens every year," says a gray-haired man with glasses. "Whenever our minutemen restage the first battle of the Revolution, some spectators forget we're only acting."

So that's it. No wonder nobody was hurt. The fight you saw was a make-believe battle to mark the anniversary of the start of America's War of Independence.

Now in the bright morning light you see cars parked up the road. You've jumped to the twentieth century!

The people here would be very surprised to know you've actually been visiting Paul Revere's time. "Thanks for the show," you tell the soldiers before turning to go.

 Jump back two hundred years and return to the last place you saw Paul Revere—at the fire on Cornhill Street. Turn to page 48.

It's a cool spring night in 1770, several weeks since you helped rescue the little girl, Mary, from the fire on Cornhill Street. You're back at the Green Dragon.

The tavern is busy, but Ebenezer Mackintosh doesn't seem to be around. You're about to leave when the shoemaker appears from behind a door at the back and walks up to you. "Where've you been?" he asks.

"Sick," you explain. "In shock."

"I thought the fire got you," says Ebenezer.

"No, I escaped just in time."

Mackintosh offers you his hand. It's the first friendly gesture he's ever made toward you. "Welcome back," he says with a smile. Then Ebenezer lowers his voice. "If you're still interested in helping the Sons of Liberty, there's a meeting tonight."

"I am, " you say without hesitation.

He winks and leads you to the door at the back of the tavern. As you open it, you're able to make out several figures hiding in the darkness of a small room.

At first you're scared—the figures look strange! But as your eyes adjust to the light, you see they are men wearing long stocking caps. Their faces are blackened with charcoal.

Ebenezer hands you a cap and some charcoal for your face. "We're going to visit a stubborn Tory gentleman," Mackintosh explains, while putting on his own disguise. "The chap's ignored our ban on British goods. He doesn't care if England taxes us till we're penniless."

The others hiss in anger. "We'll teach him!" They pick up wooden clubs and climb out one of the windows after Mackintosh.

You slip away with them to a street lined with well-kept homes and stop in front of a large stone house. Ebenezer hammers upon the door. "Anybody home?" he yells.

Someone inside opens the door but slams it shut after seeing the shoemaker's fierce expression. The other men surround the house. "*Oooo!*" they howl, thumping the building's walls with their clubs.

Smash! One of the men thrusts his club through a windowpane. "Stop buying from England, traitor!" he cries. The man is about to break another window, but a shorter member of the group stops him.

"That's enough," orders the second man.

"We're here to teach, not to destroy."

Smash! Someone on the other side of the house breaks a window. The short man runs to Mackintosh, who's pounding on the front door. "Ebenezer, they're getting out of control!" he tells him.

Lowering his club, the shoemaker whistles sharply. "The lesson's over!" he shouts. The others stop their noisemaking and gather around their leader. "Fine job, friends," Mackintosh says. "Tomorrow night we meet at Edes and Gill's."

After saluting one another, the men separate and disappear into the night.

You'd suspected Edes and Gill were part of the Sons of Liberty. Now you've seen that some of the group's members were men of violence. To fight the Revolution, America had both hotheaded and coolheaded patriots.

It's time you returned to 1773, the year of the Tea Party.

 Turn to page 73.

It's early morning, and much of Boston is still asleep.

You're standing near the site of the Cornhill Street fire. One of your sleeves is slightly singed, and your hands are black with soot. You feel groggy, but you're safe.

The burning house from which you rescued the girl is a heap of smoldering ashes. Four other neighboring homes have met the same, sad fate. You hope no one has been hurt.

Hearing the *clip-clop* of horses' hooves, you look up to see a handsome, well-dressed man riding a chestnut mare down the street. You recognize him from the Green Dragon tavern. He's one of Sam Adams's friends.

"Hello, my young friend. I thought we'd lost you in the fire," he says, surprised. "How did you escape?"

"I, uh, jumped through a hole in the back wall of the house," you reply, thinking quickly.

"We searched all over," he says. "Where did you go?" The man sounds concerned. It feels good to know you've been missed.

"I don't know. I must have fainted," you try to explain. "I woke up in the street only a few minutes ago."

The man gracefully jumps off his horse. "Allow me to examine you for a moment," he says. "Don't worry. I'm a doctor. My name is Joseph Warren."

With a very gentle touch, Dr. Warren examines your head. "Hmmm." He checks your eyes. "It's curious. You must have been walking around in shock."

"Yes! That's right," you agree quickly.

"You seem fine now, but you could certainly use one of these." He hands you a white handkerchief from his vest pocket. "You look like a chimney sweep."

You wipe off your face and hands; the cloth turns black. "How is the little girl who got caught in the fire?" you ask.

Dr. Warren shakes his head and sighs. "Mary is very weak," he says. "I have recommended warm baths, but I don't know what else to do for her except pray."

Warm baths and prayers? Is that all? Doctors during Paul Revere's time must have lost a lot of patients.

"Thanks to you she has a chance," Dr. Warren adds. "You were very heroic to go into that burning house." He mounts his horse. "I must visit two other fire victims," he says. "I hope I can be of more help to them."

You want to ask the kind doctor if his friendship with Sam Adams has brought him into contact with the Sons of Liberty, but you don't want to keep him from his patients. After bidding you good-bye, Dr. Warren rides off.

You've now met many people who probably took part in the Boston Tea Party. You wonder whether you know enough to jump ahead to the year of the famous event.

Or perhaps you should stay and find Ebenezer Mackintosh, so you can learn more about the inner workings of the Sons of Liberty.

Do you want to find Mackintosh? Turn to page 56.

Do you want to jump ahead in time to 1773? Turn to page 73.

It's nearly six o'clock on the evening of December 16, 1773. You're in front of Old South Meeting House, which is jammed with people.

Elbowing your way inside, you find Old South's huge, candle-lit hall in an uproar. "We've heard enough speeches," someone shouts from a balcony above. "We want action!"

Near you stands a schoolmaster with his students, who have probably come straight from class. He's explaining what is going on.

"The people are waiting to hear from the governor of Massachusetts," he yells so his students can hear. "They want him to grant a permit to send away the three ships at Griffin Wharf. Up until now he's refused to do it."

"Why?" asks one of the youngsters.

"The governor is a Tory. He says British law requires the ships to stay and unload," replies the teacher. "But the law is unfair. It allows England to tax us without our say-so."

"And that's tyranny!" adds a woman who's been listening to the schoolmaster. The students join in the shouting.

In the balcony you spot George Robert Twelves Hewes whistling and clapping. "Hurrah!" he yells merrily. George seems to be enjoying the meeting as if it's a big show.

In a corner opposite you crouches Ebenezer Mackintosh, fists clenched at his side. "Adjourn the meeting!" cries a rowdy group of men gathered around him. "Action! Action!"

Sam Adams is sitting calmly up front. Close by are Dr. Joseph Warren and Paul Revere, grim-faced and quiet.

Suddenly, the meeting hall falls quiet. "It's the *Dartmouth*'s owner," you hear the schoolmaster tell his students, as a finely dressed young man enters and warily makes his way up front to the podium.

"I have met with the governor," the young man announces. "He will not permit my ship to leave Boston without unloading its tea."

"Don't listen to him," advises Sam Adams, rising defiantly to his feet.

The young man sighs. "I must."

Adams shrugs. "Then there's no point in continuing this meeting."

Immediately, a piercing war-cry comes from the balcony. *"Whoop! Whoop! Whoop!"* someone answers below. As if by plan, people run to the

64

exits. "To Griffin Wharf!" voices shout. "Boston Harbor will be a teapot, tonight!"

Seeing Ebenezer Mackintosh rush out the back, you try to follow. But your way is blocked by the crowd. Paul Revere, too, hurries out a side door before you can reach him.

Look! There's Joshua, Edes and Gill's apprentice. Maybe you can catch up with him before he runs out. Or should you follow Sam Adams and Dr. Warren, who are leaving the meeting hall at a more leisurely pace? Hurry! The Tea Party is about to begin!

 Should you try to reach Joshua? Turn to page 75.

 Do you want to follow Sam Adams? Turn to page 70.

The sun is setting, and you're confused. You expected to go with Paul Revere to three ships carrying English-taxed tea. Instead, he's headed away from Boston Harbor and is now leading you across town toward the Boston Common.

"Isn't the Tea Party going to be by the docks?" you ask.

"The docks?" Paul's cheeks turn red as he laughs. His laughter, easy and full, is a pleasure to hear. "Now wouldn't that be an amusing place to see Dr. Warren's stylish wife serving tea!"

You don't understand. "Dr. Warren's wife?"

"Yes. This is for her," Revere tells you, still chuckling. Unwrapping the bundle under his arm, he shows you an elegant silver teapot decorated with a flowery crest. The name *Paul Revere* is engraved in the bottom.

"It's very beautiful," you say in admiration.

The teapot's gifted creator turns serious. "It isn't meant to hold British-taxed tea,"he tells you. "It brews only homegrown American tea."

You and Paul Revere arrive at a big, fine house near Faneuil Hall. Outside stand several horse-drawn carriages. You're in one of Boston's more exclusive neighborhoods.

A beautiful woman answers the door. "Mr. Revere!" she says. "So nice to see you."

Revere introduces you to Elizabeth Warren, who graciously invites you both inside. By now, you understand the silversmith earlier was talking about going to *a* tea party, not *the* Tea Party. But it doesn't matter. You've made friends with Paul Revere.

Women in long gaily colored dresses sit about the Warrens' salon. The room is expensively furnished with fine carpets and polished wooden furniture.

Revere presents his teapot to Elizabeth. "It's magnificent," she exclaims. The other women nod in agreement.

"I can't stay very long," the silversmith says. "But I wanted to urge you all to drink our own Labrador tea, instead of the British import. We must show England we mean business."

"Here, here!" several women say. Elizabeth Warren hands you a cup of Labrador tea. You take a sip. Yuck! It tastes like peppermint-flavored tree bark. Only a true patriot would drink such stuff.

"As we speak, several ships carrying taxed tea are sailing here from England," Revere tells the women. "Britain wants to sell us the tea. But we mustn't buy it."

"We won't!" one woman shouts. "Count on us," adds another.

"That's what I was hoping you would say. Because we have some patriots who are so angry over the tea tax they are ready to go to war right now," Paul Revere replies. Then he timidly adds, "Now, I'd better hurry home for dinner, or my wife will twist my ear off." Everybody laughs, Paul loudest of all. You can tell he's the kind of man who enjoys joking around.

After thanking Elizabeth Warren for her hospitality, you and the silversmith leave the house.

Paul Revere pats you on the back. "Come to my home for dinner," he offers. "You'll have a merry time meeting my family."

You'd love to accept, but you can't. Having won his repect, you're ready to take part in the Boston Tea Party.

"Thank you, but I must be getting home, too," you reply.

"Another time then," he says. You shake hands and part.

Now you have two choices. You can go straight to Boston Harbor. Or you can stop first in the center of town, where the Sons of Liberty may be preparing for the Tea Party.

 Do you want to go to Boston Harbor? **Turn to page 72.**

 Should you jump to the center of town? **Turn to page 62.**

You're with Sam Adams and Joseph Warren as they march down Milk Street toward Boston Harbor. Good! They're heading for Griffin Wharf.

A bright moon lights up the night sky as the three of you join a large, quiet crowd. If not for the sound of marching feet, you'd think you were in a silent movie.

Approaching Griffin Wharf, you see the pier lit up with lanterns. *Whack! Whack!* Men are cracking open wooden chests on board the three tall ships, whose riggings look like giant cobwebs against the moonlit sky.

A salty sweet aroma fills your nostrils. It's the smell of tea and salt water.

You're anxious to join the Tea Party with Sam Adams and Joseph Warren, but they just stop on the pier to watch.

"Mr. Adams, why—" you start to ask, but an elderly man hisses.

"Quiet!" he whispers angrily. "We didn't come here to talk. Another word and I'll toss you into the drink!"

It looks as if you've followed the wrong people. Many patriots such as Sam Adams and Joseph Warren only witnessed the Tea Party, instead of taking an active part in it.

On one of the ships you see a boy whose blackened face reminds you of Joshua Wyeth.

You can't simply step on board to join the Tea Party. You have no disguise. You decide to jump back to Old South Meeting House where you can find out where the participants in the Boston Tea Party are meeting.

 Turn to page 75.

You're back on Long Wharf, where you began your mission. It's December 16, 1773, the evening of the Boston Tea Party. But the pier is deserted. Where is everybody?

Cree! Cree! A lone seagull swoops out of the dark sky to scoop a fish from the water. The bird's cry and the sea lapping against Long Wharf are the only sounds you hear.

Long Wharf? In your haste you've wound up in the wrong place at the right time. The three ships carrying the British-taxed tea are moored at Griffin Wharf, not Long Wharf.

Should you jump straight to Griffin Wharf now? Or should you go to the center of town, where a meeting about the tea may be in progress?

 Do you want to jump to Griffin Wharf? Turn to page 70.

 Should you go to the center of town? Turn to page 62.

You find yourself on a busy wharf at day's end in mid-November 1773. The pier is smaller than Boston's Long Wharf, where you first arrived when you began your mission. But this place seems even livelier with sailors, peddlers, and craftsmen.

Walking along, you spot a shop with a sign that reads *Silversmith*. Coming out the door is Paul Revere!

You run up to him. "Hello, Mr. Revere."

He studies your face. "Have we met before?" he asks.

"Yes, three years ago," you explain. "The night of the Cornhill Street fire."

Paul Revere smiles at you as if you were a long lost friend. "Of course," he says. "I remember Dr. Warren telling me he saw you the next morning looking as if you had slept in a chimney. Where have you been?"

"I was living with my family in New York," you fib.

"Well, they must be proud of you. And I'm

happy to meet you again," he says. "I'm on my way to drop off something at a special tea party. Would you care to come along?"

It seems too good to be true. "I'd be delighted!" you say.

Paul Revere goes into his shop and brings out something heavy wrapped in cloth. Could it be a tomahawk?

"Let's go," he says.

Turn to page 65.

Outside the meeting hall you find complete chaos. You look around and spot Joshua's blond head not far in front of you. He edges through the mob pouring out of Old South and turns down a narrow side street.

"Wait, Joshua!" you yell, struggling to keep up. But he doesn't hear you. By the time you reach the street he's turned down, the printer's apprentice is gone.

Despite a bright moon, the night makes it difficult to tell where you are. Still, the street you're on seems familiar.

Creak! The sound of a door closing catches your attention. You run toward it and discover you're in front of Edes and Gill's printing shop! Peeking through a crack in the door, you see men putting on blankets and rubbing their faces with grease.

Excited, you enter the shop. But a stranger bars your path. "Me know you?" he asks with a grunt.

"I, uh—" you begin to say.

"No worry," says a second man nearby. "Me know this one." The second man's face is covered with soot, and his voice is disguised to sound like an Indian's. But from the look of his roughened workman's hands, you're almost sure he's Ebenezer Mackintosh.

The first man nods and hands you a dab of grease for your face, while the man who resembles Mackintosh gives you a blanket and a piece of cord to tie it across your shoulders. "Hurry!" he growls.

You dress quickly and leave the shop with the others. *"Hoo, hoo!"* a voice calls from down the street. Your group hurries toward the owl-like sound and meets up with other disguised Indians.

As all of you march in silence toward Griffin Wharf, you spot one Indian whose yellow breeches remind you of George Hewes. He must be part of the Tea Party, too.

At the pier, the three cargo ships sway in the water like sleeping sea monsters.

Two groups of Indians board the vessels that have the names *Dartmouth* and *Eleanor* painted on their sides. A short, stocky Indian on the dock signals in your direction. "Come on!" he says gruffly, leading you and the others toward the boat named *Beaver*. You're almost positive the disguised man is Paul Revere!

Once on board, some of the men use a block and tackle to hoist the chests of tea from the *Beaver's* hold. Others, including the stocky man who resembles Paul Revere, pull small tomahawks from their belts. *Whack! Whack!* Their Boston-made tomahawks glimmer in the moonlight as they split apart the heavy wooden crates.

Your job is to help dump the tea overboard. "Take!" says the stocky man, offering you a broom. Now you are also responsible for sweeping off any tea that falls on the deck.

It's hard work, and soon you're sweating. Dry tea leaves cling to your wet skin and fly up your nose. They make your eyes tear, and your head feels light.

Hundreds of people on Griffin Wharf watch in total silence. Except for an occasional Indianlike grunt, nobody on board the three ships says anything, either.

After hours of dumping and sweeping tea, your arms are ready to fall off.

When the last crate is finally tossed overboard, you sigh in relief. The harbor is filled with so many broken crates that it seems you could walk from one to another without getting wet.

The stocky man drops his tomahawk on the

Beaver's deck. "Good work, Sons of Liberty," he says in a gravelly voice.

The object of your mission lies five feet away! You pick up the tomahawk, which feels warm and smells of tea. "Keep it," says the man, smiling. His teeth look white as milk in the middle of his grease-covered face. You proudly follow him and the others off the boat.

Congratulations! You've witnessed Paul Revere's role in the Boston Tea Party and you've earned your tomahawk. Most important, you've played a part in America's struggle for independence.

Winning freedom from England will be the patriots' next big step!

Mission Completed.

About the Contributors

MARC KORNBLATT, a former actor, has worked as staff reporter for two Manhattan weekly newspapers as well as freelancing for the New York *Daily News*. He is the co-author of Time Machine #11, *Mission to World War II*, and author of Time Machine #15, *Flame of the Inquisition*.

ERNIE COLÓN has worked in many styles and media in his thirty-year professional career. His work has appeared in children's books, comic books, and magazines. He has drawn Casper the Friendly Ghost and Richie Rich for Harvey Publications and is presently illustrating fantasy and science fiction for DC Comics. He is the illustrator of Time Machine #13, *Secret of the Royal Treasure*.